TODAY YOU HOLD MY HAND

written by Erin Winters

Illustrations and cover design by Kaitin Röckle

Hardback ISBN: 978-1-958702-31-4
Paperback ISBN: 978-1-958702-30-7

SNOWFALL
PUBLICATIONS LLC

To August and Gideon,
who still hold my hand,
but grow bigger every day.

Daddy and I are so proud of you.
We love you.

Today a hug can solve it all
No matter quite how hard you fall
Today you want me at your side
For every bug, for every slide
Today you hold my hand.

Today you run at me full speed
To show me that you found a weed
Today you cackle upside-down
And wave away a sorry frown

Today you hold my hand.

Today you sing your favorite song
You've made it last twelve verses long
Today you gather sticks and rocks
And skip down to our blue mailbox
Today you hold my hand.

Today you drive your matchbox cars
You go to sleep and dream of Mars
Today you twirl around until
You roll and giggle down the hill
Today you hold my hand.

Today you tell me all about
The seed that grows a little sprout
Today it's small, but in the light

In time, like you, it gains its might
Today you hold my hand.

Today the mornings bring a bright
And smiling visage to my sight!
You grin at nine, and cry by ten
Repeat a thousand times, and then
Today you hold my hand.

Today we tire, you and I,
Sometimes we let out quite a sigh
Today our feelings feel so wild
Nothing's ever really mild
Today you hold my hand.

Today we do what's done before
We fight, we snuggle, we endure
Today we love so very deep
No matter what, from wake to sleep
Today you hold my hand.

Today when fog is thick outside
You wonder with eyes big and wide

If clouds are low, or we are high
And if we'll ever see the sky
Today you hold my hand.

Today your stories bring me joy
Each silly mischief trick and ploy

Today chalk drawings on the street
Pair beautifully with padding feet
Today you hold my hand.

Today's a day I love to hold
To freeze in time, no growing old
Today's a day I squeeze you tight
I'm here to tuck you in at night
Today you hold my hand.

Someday I might embarrass you
Your problems will be bigger, too
Someday a kiss won't fix it all
Such big adventures will befall

But...
Today you hold my hand.

GET A FREE FEELINGS CHART

A tool for parents, caregivers, and clinicians.

Everyone has emotions! Sometimes it is hard to know what we are feeling and why. Learning about our emotions and talking about them with someone safe can help. This free resource is a great way to engage children in learning emotional regulation skills.

SCAN ME

Erin Winters is a Licensed Professional Counselor, mom, and founder of Snowfall Publications LLC. Erin uses her clinical knowledge and experience to write high quality therapeutic children's books normalizing emotions and promoting mental health.

Erin has worked in a variety of mental health settingss including a child and adolescent psychiatric unit at a hospital, intensive in-home therapy, substance abuse programs for adults, and currently works in an outpatient setting with a variety of client ages, struggles, and goals.

When she isn't working or writing, Erin loves spending time with her husband and their two little boys, reading novels, and drinking hot chocolate.

OUR LATEST ADVENTURES

snowfallpublications.com

Printed in Great Britain
by Amazon

57440646R00018